To Madeline: Your love of the word *no*, your loving obstinacy,
and your love for me are the reasons why this book exists.

—ML

Henry, may you always shout animal facts at anyone who will listen
from behind a (sometimes) closed bathroom door. Rosie, may you always
work as hard as you do to prove him wrong. Thor, I love you—more.

—SJ

For my kids.

—JC

ABOUT THIS BOOK

The illustrations in this book finally got done because Jared's dad kept bugging him. "Have you worked on that spread with the alligator yet?" "The beetle isn't going to draw himself, you know!" It went on and on. But when his dad wouldn't let him watch TV until he finished his work, Jared sat down at his computer and created the art digitally in Photoshop. And even though his dad can be annoying, Jared is glad he's his dad.

This book was edited by Connie Hsu and Deirdre Jones and designed by Phil Caminiti under the art direction of Saho Fujii. The production was supervised by Erika Schwartz, and the production editor was Christine Ma. This book was printed on 128 gsm Gold Sun Matte. The text was set in Avenir Next, and the display type was Potato Cut.

BE GLAD YOUR DAD...

Is Not an Octopus!

Written by

MATTHEW LOGELIN
and SARA JENSEN

Art by JARED CHAPMAN

Little, Brown and Company

New York   Boston

Most of the time, you're
glad your dad is your dad,

like when he's telling funny stories,

singing silly songs,

or letting you jump on the bed.

But you're probably not
glad your dad is your dad

when he's grouchy, bossy, or just totally gross.

And sometimes you wish your dad were...anything but him!

But be careful what you wish for
because it could be way worse....

Be glad your dad is not a DOG, because he would lick your face to say hello.

Be glad your dad is not an **OWL**,
because he would keep you
up AAAAAAAAALL night.

Be glad your dad is not an IGUANA,
because he would puff up and hiss at you when he was grumpy.

Be glad your dad is not a SKUNK,
because he would make you so stinky when you surprised him.

Be glad your dad is not a **TORTOISE**,

because

EVERYTHING

WOULD TAKE FOREVER.

Be glad your dad is not a **PEACOCK**, because he would think that he was so much prettier than you.

Be glad your dad is not a SNAKE, because he would shed his skin in front of your friends.

Be glad your dad is not an **ALLIGATOR**,

because he would have tons of extremely sharp teeth

(AND PROBABLY REALLY BAD BREATH).

Be glad your dad is not a DUNG BEETLE, because he would pile poop in your room. (Seriously, that would be really gross.)

Be glad your dad is not a WHALE,

because
you
couldn't
take
him
ANYWHERE!

Be glad your dad is not a MONKEY, because he would make you eat bugs (and they might get stuck in your teeth).

Be glad your dad is not an OCTOPUS, because he would always win at tag.

You're both it!

Be glad your dad is not a **UNICORN**, because no one would believe you.

Be glad your dad is not a **QUAIL** , because he would be so boring.

So you should be glad your dad is your dad, because he will probably never do any of these crazy things (like pile poop in your room).

And he will always love you more than anything,
anything in the whole wide world...

...even if he is kind of annoying.

MORE ABOUT THE ANIMALS IN THIS BOOK

WHY DO DOGS LICK FACES?

Dogs lick faces to say "hello" or "sorry." (And sometimes it's just a gross kiss.)

WHY DO OWLS KEEP THEIR KIDS UP ALL NIGHT?

Many species of owls hunt at night because the animals that they eat are more plentiful when it's dark. (As a night owl, you would never get the first worm.)

WHY DO IGUANAS PUFF UP AND HISS?

Iguanas have lots of natural predators, and to scare them off, iguanas puff up and hiss. (You will never hear an iguana dad say to his kids, "Use your words.")

WHY DO SKUNKS MAKE YOU STINKY?

When a skunk is surprised, it sprays a smelly liquid to scare away predators. Skunks would prefer to save their stink for special occasions, though, because it takes them several days to make more of it. (Skunk dads would hate a surprise party.)

WHY ARE TORTOISES SO SLOW?

Many scientists believe that tortoises are super slow because they don't have to chase their food (they're herbivores, which means they eat plants) and because they don't have to run from most predators (their shells protect them). (Their shells also give them a place to hide when their kids annoy them.)

WHY DO PEACOCK DADS THINK THEY'RE PRETTIER THAN YOU?

Have you seen their tail feathers? Peacocks fan those beautiful things to attract the attention of females. Males are called peacocks while females are called peahens and babies are called peachicks. Together they're called peafowl. (Tell your friends.)

WHY DO SNAKES SHED THEIR SKIN?

Snakes shed layers of their skin (this is called "molting") a few times every year to remove gross stuff like parasites or to get rid of their old, damaged skin. (Your dad should change his clothes every day.)

WHAT'S THIS ABOUT ALLIGATOR TEETH?

Alligators will go through two thousand to three thousand teeth in their lifetimes and never have to go to the dentist. In your lifetime, you will have only fifty-two teeth and will go to the dentist about 160 times. (Doesn't seem fair, does it?)

WHY ARE BEES ALWAYS BUZZING?

Bees' wings move really, really quickly (over two hundred beats per second), which causes that buzzing sound. Male bees don't have stingers and are sometimes called drones. The authors of this book advise you to stay away from female bees, which are sometimes called workers. (Dad bees may be annoying, but at least they won't sting you.)

WHY ARE DUNG BEETLES SO DISGUSTING?

Sure, dung beetles pile up poop and eat it. If they didn't, the whole world would be covered in the stuff! But did you know that dung beetles are one of the few animals (besides humans) that navigate by using the stars? (So they're equally disgusting and awesome, just like your dad.)

WHY CAN'T YOU TAKE YOUR WHALE DAD ANYWHERE?

Whales are the largest mammals on Earth. Some of them are nearly as large as a space shuttle! (So I guess maybe you could take your whale dad to outer space.)

YOU THINK YOUR DAD IS OLD?

Dinosaurs became extinct sixty-five million years before your dad was even born. (If you like dinosaurs, go to your local museum and see their bones, and if you really, really like dinosaurs, you should become a paleontologist.)

WHY DO MONKEYS EAT BUGS?

Monkeys snack on bugs because bugs are a great source of protein. (The authors of this book would rather eat edamame.)

WHY WOULD AN OCTOPUS WIN EVERY GAME OF TAG?

An octopus has eight arms. (And it is probably smarter than you.)

ARE UNICORNS REAL?

Unicorns live only in books. Open up as many books as you can to find one (and so much more).

TELL ME SOMETHING MORE ABOUT QUAIL.

Quail are still boring.